Heart Escapades

Heart Escapades

CHRISELLE. J. FERNANDES

PARTRIDGE
A Penguin Random House Company

To order additional copies of this book, contact
Partridge India
000 800 10062 62
orders.india@partridgepublishing.com

www.partridgepublishing.com/india

Contents

1. Playground 1
2. Wanton Kid 3
3. Heart 5
4. Beyond Means 7
5. Misty Goodbyes No More 9
6. Frivolous Love Feelings 11
7. That Night 13
8. A Night With A Stranger 15
9. Lost Again 17
10. Jump 19
11. Sometimes in Fleeting Moments 21
12. I Am Going To Miss You A Little Less Every Day 23
13. Love 25
14. The One Who Overdid Don't 27
15. Late Night Musings 29
16. Double edged 31
17. Magic in Motion 33
18. Remembering You 35
19. The Fall- Again 37
20. The Game We Play 39
21. Forget Me Not 43
22. Next Time 45
23. Sometimes 47
24. Sometimes ii 49
25. And I keep falling 51
26. No 53
27. Of Bright Sunshines and Dark Desires 55
28. Answers Abound 57

29. Together Alone..59

30. Let's play a game... 61

31. It's Not Goodbye....................................63

32. Today..65

33. Muse...67

34. Muse ii..69

35. I'm sorry..71

36. My Plea...73

37. Traces...75

38. Lest 77

39. Fuel..79

40. Sometimes iii 81

41. Sometimes iv...83

42. Messages From the Lost World Care 85

43. The Unrequited..................................... 87

44. Black and Blue 89

45. The Search..91

46. I Hope You Don't Mind..........................93

47. Lasting Summer.................................... 95

48. Cut... 97

49. I Love You Unlike 99

50. I'm Tired.. 101

51. Just One Touch................................... 103

52. Rattlemind.. 105

53. Un-Fool Me 107

54. Begin Again 109

55. Just like the others.............................. 111

56. The Meet.. 113

57. Leave Him 115

58. I wonder.. 117

In mirth of those who have
not forgotten me and
In memory of those who have.

****

59

The old
Feel the need to explain, classify
And brand
They teach their young to do the same
But the rebellious ones,
On rare moons,
Feed on such spontaneous sparks of insanity
Like howling wolves
Thirsty
The end is yet to be seen
Either a drop of precious elixir
Or the salty water of the vast ocean.

****

***

1

Playground

Your heart is like a playground
With lovers swinging in and out
In and out
Whizzing by in your merry- go- round
Wind in their hair,
Sparkling eyes, wistful bright toothed smiles.
Climbing in and sliding out,
Along your slippery tongue
But when its gets dark and cold,
And your steel soul fails to warm,
All the swingers, whizzers and sliders go
Home.

***

***

2

Wanton Kid

Eyes glistening with desire, she pleaded
"Please, let me!"
I looked away. I disapproved.
It wasn't time yet.
All around and elsewhere lights twinkled
And music played. But we were oblivious.
She persisted. I stood my ground.
Desire changed to need.
A tear rolled down her cheek.
I felt her yearn
And yet
I couldn't let her
On the ferris wheel.
The kid, I was certain
wasn't ready for its intensity.

***

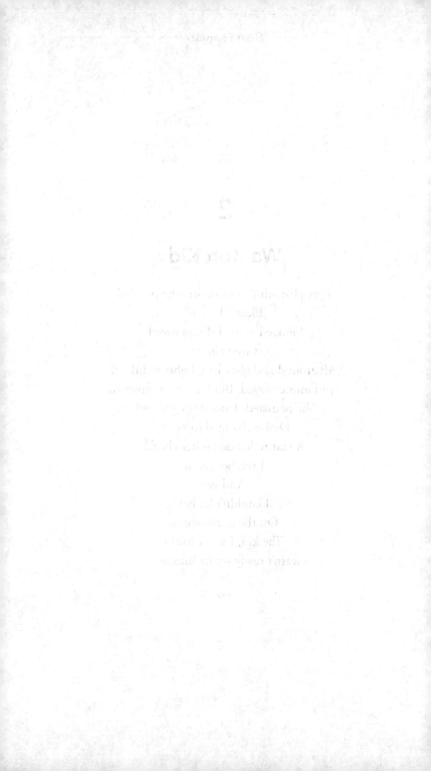

***

 **3**

Heart

I
live
through
your eyes, your body, your movements
For
In
You
My soul is
either ravaged or nourished.
I seek you not
For worldly pleasures
but for a joy uncontained in a tiny jar called
Heart.

***

***

4

Beyond Means

My darkness is your light
And your light is a mystery.
If I'd only known,
I would not seek you
To lose myself.
Do you then revel in my misery?
Yours are sunlight kissed eyes
Mine hollow, yearn for summer rain,
Yours are red wined doused lips
Mine are parched and parted
Your tongue speaks of wisdom from another world
Mine utters sighs and moans
Your body is effervescent
Mine is a corpse.
I still follow you
A wanderer in rapture
Of a colourful fluttering butterfly in
a green sky and blue hills.

***

***

5

Misty Goodbyes No More

This time I didn't cry,
Neither did you.
I must be getting good at goodbyes
or maybe we are not close, enough.

This time we didn't speak much,
We didn't promise
We didn't hug,
We stretched our hands out and shook them
like businessmen do,
on greeting one another.
This time we didn't hold on longer either,
Our hands were not intertwined
Like lovers, neither more than friends
It seemed like a passing time between the change of a season,
That unsettling time.

This time, our eyes didn't linger on,
We did not whisper the good
We didn't not speak about the bad,
We didn't reminiscence.
This time it didn't hurt as much
My eyes did not weep,
My heart didn't ache as usual,
I did not trace your footsteps.

I instead quietened my restless soul
With a stony unwavering stare at the television screen
Later that evening.
My eyes moist.
Throat parched.
With unsaid words,
Never destined to part.

***

***

6

Frivolous Love Feelings

I love you
Then I hate you
I love you
Then I hate you again.
I love you again.
And I love you
Because I simply do.
There is no reason.
And it infuriates me that I do not
have a reason for loving you.
I love you.
FOR,
I think of you in the in-betweens of humdrum life
While climbing long winding stairs,
On lonely streets with the moon facing bare,
In the silences of the night,
In the noise of the train chugging,
When its piercing whistle sounds
the foggy morning,
When the rain hits the heated ground,
When the air is filled with the aroma of
of sweet earth.
When the trees sway to the strong winds
When the leaves rustle and the black birds dot the grey sky
When the sun shines on a balmy afternoon
When twilight is nigh.

When the tiny squirrel runs down the spine
of the shady tree
I think of you and me.
I think of hammocks and swings
Of winds blowing tresses
Of having fun
I think of beaches and exploring unfamiliar lands
listening to music together of eclectic bands.

And so for all this thinking and feeling,
I think
I must be in love.
Unless these in-betweens cease
I will love-hate you unconditionally
for reasons unfound.

***

***

7

That Night

It seems long ago now,
Although it isn't.
A faint memory
That keeps popping
Every now and then
Just for an instant.

My heart leaps,
Pictures peep into its windowed chambers
I replay it in my mind
For I fear
I might forget
I might lose the fluttering butterfly
And the accompanying fever

Inebriation has its faults,
and flaws grow a plenty
And I would have had you sober
But societal inhibitions create barriers.

So I'll remember it
Like I do now,
passionate, spontaneous
haphazard, and quick
Good, free-falling,
Short and un-satiated.
Wanting more.

***

***

8

A Night With A Stranger

I looked at the stars that night
And felt one with the sky
I didn't care you were a stranger
I didn't ask why
You held my hand and then
held me tight
With your arm wrapped around my back,
Secure, you sold me an idea and
I laughed silently

It was a moonless night
Filled with stars
With slight breeze to intersperse the
crashing waves and the silence
I hung onto you dear stranger
And would have believed you even if you lied

And though we may never meet again
I know I felt safe
On a hot summer's night
Near the surge
Reckless decisions
Undertaken
Happily

Stranger we were bonded by
uncertainty and
the threads of fun and surprise
And a certain intensity;
This elation I cannot, now, seem to hide.

But since I have to be sane now
and be worried what people would think
I'll head home and pretend
This never happened
But secretly hoping
This is not the end
of our secret rendezvous.

***

***

9

Lost Again

We've lost ourselves again
You and I
In our own worlds of reality
Of ego and downfall.

We've lost ourselves again
You and I
And this time it is better
To stay that way
You say
It is better never
to find us again.

We've lost ourselves for good.
In this dense wood.
Where lies don't hold ground
Where we've stabbed and squeezed
Out anything that would have helped us
Climb toward light.
We've surrounded ourselves with
Just the cries of a haunting past
Delusions and insecurities and
Unrequited love.

We've lost ourselves again
You and I
And this time it's better we
Stay lost.
For it is the only way
To live now
Stuck in a constant limbo
Of what was and what will be.
Lost has never been so freeing.

***

***

10

Jump

I desire to jump now,
Only because you did,
And she did,
And he did.
And they did.

I desire to jump now,
Not knowing if I really want to.

I desire to jump and
Feel the air
Brush against my face

When I take the plunge
Not knowing if this surge
Is going to last.

I desire to jump now,
Only because I feel
My time has come
Or it has passed!

I desire to jump now,
Still not knowing
where
how
or with whom.

I desire to jump now,
Knowing some might say
It was too soon.

***

***

11

Sometimes in Fleeting Moments

This feels like I've been here before,
But
Whisper in my ear,
And I will forget
The time passed by.

I will live with you in this
Moment
Kiss me on my neck
And I will forget
Everyone else.

Breathe and let your heart beat with
Mine
Closer closer closer together
Until I feel your passion
In my veins.

Two have never be in such wonderful
Rhythm
Like now.

One has never been such
Fun
Until now.

Exhaustion has never been so
Exhilarating
Until now.

***

***

12

I Am Going To Miss You A Little Less Every Day

Piece by piece you marked your territory
Like a little child who knows
not of the complications of possession
With a violent storm
And a magical mystery
You stole what was mine
And I willingly let you
plunder my world asunder
Even though you smirk with pride
Basking in your achievement
I know
I am going to miss you a little less every day.

Faster than sand in that decadent yellow time glass
Swifter than the slow starch and certain skill
With which you pillaged my wealth and ruined me
Drank off me and fed off me.

You left without a second glance
Without waiting for a little longer
But I knew I was going to miss you a little less everyday
You rode without wonder on a horse wind so strong
And ceased to be the revered mystic traveler

Illusions could be poison and maim
But rebirth could enliven even the dead
Years hence after all is forgotten.
You will return and I will cease to remember
And the motes that trickle though the crannies
Of my once magnificent temple walls
Will raze you.

***

13

Love

It feels like fever
A headiness bereft of inebriation
Blood gushing in a vortex of a thousand veins
To and fro
Electrifying each sense
Demanding a cessation
To a spontaneous bedlam of emotions
And deliverance comes
In an opportunity
On winding stairs
Enfolding arms
An intense moment-
Caught in time,
A secret embrace
Has never been so
Gratifying.

***

***

14

The One Who Overdid Don't

I don't think you love me,
I don't think you care,
You might tell me otherwise with a certain earnestness,
But behind the caring façade
I see, I see the snare.

What makes you think like that?
Of course you ask me,
And throw a bit of reverse psychology,
To scare me into accepting defeat.

But don't my mind know better?
And don't my mind know me?

So don't I know?
You don't love me anymore,
And that you like someone new.
You didn't call or text,
Even though you're busy excuse
Could have actually been true.

I don't want to hear any explanations,
I don't want to talk,
I don't want you to raise your voice,
I don't want to be stuck.

I don't want to wish and wonder if,
I don't want to wait and hope,
I don't want to be disheartened
Because I know that you won't come for me
When I tumble from the winding slope.
Because,

Don't I know?

***

***

15

Late Night Musings

I looked and at once was drawn to you,
Again.
You were pale yet beautiful,
Incomplete yet perfect.
You were there
as if you never changed.

I watched raptured and
Trapped you in a playful gaze.
No trace of warmth
but a cold yet shy welcoming song made its way to me.
I marveled at my sudden madness whilst
The half moon glistened amidst the slits
Of coconut tree leaves.

***

***

16

Double edged

Drained
Out of my insecurities and

Hurt
By reality's stake, deeply

Burdened
For the choice I have to make is

Grave
As it cuts me more, within my

Soul
To keep me away from you is

Difficult
For this decision is double edged and I.

Die
Both ways.

***

***

17

Magic in Motion

When feet match the rhythm
Of the music that grows
Louder .Louder .
Thumping
Like the stars blinking in disbelief
Like the dark night wearing on
Darker. Darker.
Waking
The dawn's drooping eyelids.
I see you,
Magic in motion.

***

***

18

Remembering You

I already miss you,
And you haven't left.
Is that a sign of acceptance?
Or a sign of early grief?
I do not want to wait,
I do not want you to go.

I want you to change your mind,
Before I look for another kind.
I want you to be there.
I want you to care.
I don't want to miss you,
When you still haven't left.

***

***

19

The Fall- Again

Here we are,
At it again.
Where we picked up
From last time.

The same
words spoken,
bitterness,
loneliness and heartache.
And the uneasy silence.

This time I hope it is the last time.
This time I wish for a quiet calm.
A peaceful state of being.
Without the unnecessary questions
That make me a disheveled fool.

Are you still with me in spirit?
Do you still think about me?
Have you gone ahead with living the way you want to?
Did you ever love me?
Why

is my reality still connected with yours
When you have given up on us?
Why do I crave for your light
when you have nothing to give me but
Darkness and despair?
Perhaps I never loved you,
As you did too.
Perhaps I imagined it all
And so this is nothing but a
Scratch on the knees fall.

***

***

20

The Game We Play

You
Run around run around
Run around me
Encircle me.
Drive me insane.
I try to catch you
But oh
You run, you run. Away.
Oh! I hate this game you play.

You
Run around run around
Run around me
Encircle me.
And almost hold me.
I get dizzy,
I try to catch you,
But oh you run away. Away.
Oh! I hate this game you play.

You,
Run around, run around
Run around me.
But I'm no where to be found.
No one to encircle.
No one to almost hold.
No one to make crazy.
No one to make dizzy.
Oh! You hate this game I play.

***

***

21

Forget Me Not

Forget me not
Tick tock
Goes the clock
It's only half a minute past,
Since you told me our love
Would not last.

Forget me not.
Tick Tock
Goes the Clock.
It's only been a week,
Since we did part,
And I still feel weak.

Forget me not.
Tick Tock
Goes the Clock.
It's only been a month,
And a while since we spoke, laughed or joked,
And I still remember you,

Forget me not.
Tick Tock
Goes the Clock.
I have lost track of time,
Spiralling out of control,
Insidiously laughing and crying.

Forget me not.
Tick Tock
Goes the Clock Not.

***

***

22

Next Time

(A little advice)

Next Time
Love me
with courage
of a 'lil more than a fly.

Next time,
Don't let love
Be swatted
By the hands of a clock.

Next time,
Worry not.
A lot.

Next time,
Love me with ardour,
With a certain belief,
That we are most certainly meant to be.

Then, perhaps,

Next time,
Our love will not cease
But move freely as naturally
As we the air breathe.

Next time.

***

***

23

Sometimes

Sometimes the days are longer
And the nights seem longer still
My breath heavier
My vision blurred
My body hopelessly grapples
Onto the fringes of a make believe reality
Until the storm of a thousand beats in my heart
Have cleared the mist in my mind
And I see you clarity
Naked
but

true.

***

***

 **24**

Sometimes ii

Sometimes the last time is just the first
A broken heart mended by time and forgetfulness
Illusions and distortions collide with reality
In a cesspool of deceit
No more does the truth reek
of lies, hurt and mind games.
Sometimes the last time is one of many times.
to come.

***

***

25

And I keep falling

And I keep falling
I've strayed away from you my love

The glistening lake beckons
Singing sweet voices of seduction
Enveloping me in white ice sheets

This strong wind
Makes me fly in a wordless world
A delightful diorama of colours-
blue, green, pink
red black
I'm lost
I'm found.
Strange musings of a wonder forlorn
Voices speak in tongues unknown

I've strayed away from you my love,

And I keep falling.

***

***

 **26**

No

I should not speak about it
stitch my mouth
with a silken smile
And let
No words
No sound
No cry
Come out of it.
Stifle the *tearidea*
For it would be as lifeless
Out
As Within

Its first breath would be its last
It would fall on earth but not grow
Creation wasted on an afterthought of

No.

***

***

27

Of Bright Sunshines
and Dark Desires

I want to sing to you
Songs of love and passion
I want to look into your eyes
While I do it
I want to feel your body
My hand entwined in yours
I want to sing to you
And see you smile
I want to touch your face
Pull your short hair
And gaze at you for a while.

I want to sing to you
Breathless at the core
While the breeze of lust flows
I want to sing for you
Only for you
For you and I
Live on sandy ground
It will sink any moment
And we will fall deliriously
Into fused feelings of nothingness and everything

I want to sing for you
While we are in the moment now
I want to make you mine
When we are here now

I want to sing to you about
Of bright sunshines and dark desires
Of beaches upon mountain tops
Of snow receding from shorelines

I want to sing to about
You and I
And how we will eventually
Fall into the hollow moon of delight.

***

***

28

Answers Abound

I know the answer
To your question.

I know the lie you tell yourself
To keep your mind satisfied.

I know the misery you are in
To keep me protected

I know how it will kill you,
To know I'm no longer there.

I know the answer
To your unasked question.

I know the answer
To my question as well.

I know I do not want to answer them
For I'm in waiting

Either the questions or time
might change.

***

***

29

Together Alone

In the darkness of the night,
A string of sweat trickling down my head,
I toss and turn and thirst,
For air,
As the wind blows the other way.
I sleep with you,
but onto one side.
Hoping not to disturb,
The snoridden lullaby.

Together alone.
Aren't we always
Together alone?

I stand at the sea shore,
And hug you at the waist,
We look at the expansive sea before us,
Our bodies and souls entwined in a wistful embrace.

Our minds and thoughts though run amock,
We think of nothing and then perhaps take stock.
We don't break the solitude in reality
but in our consciousness
It is already marred by a thousand different questions.

Together Alone,
Aren't we always
Together Alone?

***

***

30

Let's play a game...

Let's play a love game,
You and I,
Let's start what we finished
A long time ago,
When we were friends
And kissed under a cherry tree,
Tall promises and things that were
Not meant to be.
A friendship that died,
While a remorseful love lived.

Let's play a love game,
You and I,
Let's pick up where we left off,
Under the cherry tree,
And go backwards,
Let's not kiss,
Let's not make those
Tall promises and things that were
Not meant to be.

Let's play a game
Not of love,
Not of despair,
Not of degradation
Not of humiliation.

Let's play a game
Or let's not play a game.
Who are we kidding right?
We cut the cherry tree a long time ago,
Those promises of both friendship and love were pseudo,
So there's no turning back now.
and nothing to look forward to.

Let's play a game then
Of hide and seek,
A different take
Where we shall both hide and
And never seek
Each other out,
Cutting the pretense
Each hanging on to one's own sanity and desirable reality.

***

***

31

It's Not Goodbye

It's not goodbye,
Even though I have said the word.
It's not goodbye,
As I still think of you throughout the day.

It's just a farce,
To get over what you said.
It's not goodbye,
For I feel a call ringing by.
I swear

It's not goodbye.
It was never goodbye.

***

***

32

Today

Today I think I will live

Today I think I won't be consumed by you,
Your hurt.

Today I think I will survive
The onslaught of practicality,
Of truth.

Today I think I will smile,
And not because of you,
Your humour.

Today I think I will forget
and live like you
Never existed.

Just today. I think.

***

***

33

Muse

I sought you out,
Moulded you like clay,
But I should have known better,
I should have known that
You would've yelled 'Nay'
You prefer being crumpled and sordid
night or day.

You were a beautiful sculpture,
Artistically crafted to perfection,
The impurities too made for
A divine perception.
Maybe I worked too hard on you,
For you fell down and
Broke into two.

Heart mine ached,
And it still pines today,
For my handy-works gone
My grace taken away.
I should have known better than
To trust my heart,
Now torn,
A love's lost.

While I sit forlorn,
And wonder what would have been,
If I had not chosen to sculpt you?
If I had not chosen to be your queen?
You lie in heap of nothingness,
Cold and alone.
Finally being what you always wanted to be,
Half man and half stone
To the world, completely unknown.

***

***

34

Muse ii

You inspire me,
Even when you are not around,
To pen my thoughts
And think out loud.

You inspire me to forget myself
My work, my life, my duties,
And think of only you,
You who are my strife.

You inspire me dear,
With courage unknown,
To beat you up,
Even when you are not alone.

You inspire me,
To concoct situations in my head,
And make a delicious recipe,
For death.

You inspire me,
To cry daily without fail
To unlearn my experiences
And laugh in pain.

You inspire me
To do nothing to you,
For I am powerless
Without you.

You. Inspire. Me

***

***

35

I'm sorry

I'm sorry I've forgotten how to
love,
The kind that true lovers do,
I've been blinded by the world
Into accepting mediocrity
Over extraordinary
Pining for glossy
over rustic
Wanting perfect
Over real
I feel your white magic and
Our chemistry is astounding
But I take it to be an illusion
That will eventually fade
Like a late long kiss goodnight
After a lust-filled lullaby
Burned by the morning sunlight
I'm sorry I've forgotten how to
love
the kind that true lovers do.

***

***

36

My Plea

Find me
before I lose my way
Catch me
before I fall into a ceaseless pit
of self deception and remorse
Where my illusions
are my only reality
Stop me
before I leave
as I may never come back
Hold me
before I slip away
like the sands of time.

Don't rant of the futility of reality
Don't explain what went wrong
Whose fault was it,
Why we never had a song,
Don't reason,
Don't blame,
Don't ridicule,
Don't judge,

Is it too much to ask?
To quieten my myriad of thoughts with soft lullaby
About the moon and the stars!
Is it too much to ask?
To keep me smiling and alive
before I close my eyes.

***

***

37

Traces

Traces of faded memories
bind my thoughts
and deeds
Towards you my heart
leaps no more.

I try to forge the
once sired bond,
But it fails me
now since I've seen
who you really are

Nothing but someone
who feeds on my
goodness shall not
cease me to believe
in love because of your betrayal.

Innocent child I,
whirled around your idiocracies,
Until I merged into oblivion
White hazy lines and
Me no more a lot

Of tears and dreams shattered
Wisened though since before.
I hang onto the traces,
More good than bad for in those gloomy
hours I'd rather feel happier
than sad to part.

***

***

38

Lest

I am afraid now
to live by
Anyone's rules but mine.

Lest you should turn me into an
animal

Lest I should become less
human.

Lest I should forget about
myself

Lest I should remember only
you.

Lest I should cease to know what I once
was

Lest I should be someone who will never ever
laugh.

I'm afraid now
to live by
Anyone's rules but mine.

Lest I should become
undone.

***

***

39

Fuel

Fuel the red in my soul,
the tiny specks of delight,
to engulf me completely.

Upturn my magnificently dressed boat
With mighty sails and colourful banners,
But only on stormy seas.

Fuel the yellow of my being
Let the rays tingle my fingers,
My feet sting, the ground it walks on
And sink in deep in the infinite grains of sand

Guide the gushing waters
To fill up the hollow
And overwhelm me.
I cannot be contained anymore.

Fuel the lightness of light,
Let me breathe the salty air of in one last puff
Of foamy cloud,
And bathe in white.

***

***

40

Sometimes iii

Sometimes I wonder if I'd miss you,
If you'd not gone away.
If I'd feel the same way
If you were in front of me?
Absence does make the heart grow fonder.
But how much more
Would I have to wait
To hope that my feelings
Have set a good bait?
For you to pounce and devour.

Would you do so too?
or be dense like a thick forest?
where my screams could not shake even a leaf
Would you budge from
your stance
If you were still here?
or would we remain the same
In between
Grey
Not here
Not there?

Sometimes I wonder,
If it is better forgotten
I wonder if I should move on
And leave you in the shadows
Where I'd never find you again
In a mirror maze of
Fantasy
Thinking of the possible Throes of
ecstasy
Which now could never
be.

***

***

41

Sometimes iv

Sometimes I wish
I was weak enough
So that you could take me in your arms
And I surrender to your lovely charms.

Sometimes I wish
I was weak enough
So that you could save me time and again,
And I flatter your brawn and brain.

Sometimes I wish
I was weak enough
So that I could not care if you were pseudo
And I'd accept you anyhow.

Sometimes I wish
I was weak enough
So that I would cry wolf,
Each time you'd break my heart and runaway.
Rationalizing that someone had abducted you.
And hope for your return.

Sadly,
I'm not weak enough.

***

***

42

Messages From the Lost World Care

Now you may not like this
But I have a message to deliver
No? Please just listen,
I am your friend first,
You know.

I love you,
I know you won't believe it.
I do not hate you,
I know you won't believe it,
I care for you,
I know you won't believe it.

But,
Please .Just. Listen.

snap

Why do you say this?
You ask.
Why do you pretend to be connected?
You judge.
Why do you talk in an odd fashion?
You snigger.

What is wrong with you?
You point.
How do you know that?
You investigate.
What do you want in return?
You interrogate.
There is something wrong with you.
You concur.

slam

I stand still, fully aware,
That I might not be welcome any more.
I hope you just heard me out even so.
Because all that I have said
Is of love and with love,
From above.
where angels dance and
heavenly bodies abide.
Oh please won't you take the message
In your stride?

***

***

43

The Unrequited

A little love is all I ask,
No I actually ask for a lot.
And I know that I will forget what
You did to me.

The moment I get out
With the boys and girls
They don't show their true colours
Well neither do I
And nor do you.

We hide in the shadows,
Beneath the pale moon
We wait for none to be there
All to go home,
Then we lay down near the
bushes and take it slow, eventually
We will lie together helpless and nude,
There amidst no prude.

Oh touch beckons oh sweet touch
I can only wait, so much.

But No! Tough Luck!
It has rained,
Around the bushes there is muck
And while it doesn't bother me
It does you,
I'd rather have you take me in the mud
then at home in a flower bud

There is a thud and then nothing.
There is only one shadow in the pale moonlight
who is now kissing herself goodnight.

***

***

 **44**

Black and Blue

When weary meets well,
My heart begins to swell
With ache
Why have you had me break
my life into shards of glass?
Black and Blue
Black and Blue.

I walk,
I walk on them
Black and Blue
Without any remorse,
Mildly aware of the fact,
That it is life I lack.

I walk onward,
To *NoW*here.
And then to someplace Strange,
I feel colours again
All of them

Rather than
Black and Blue
Black and Blue.

***

***

45

The Search

I was searching, for something familiar,
the fuzziness, the warmth
the feeling of friendliness
but instead
I found an old bag of bones
Dirty linen and loose threads

All this while I was falling apart

I searched for support
for a transport of tranquility
but instead discovered an uneasiness
was it always like this?
was it me who had the warmth
enough for both?

Could I have been that blind?
or all the heart within you is gone?
And all that remains is a string of
pearls woven on cheap thread?

I searched for something that is no longer there
Something that now gives me a mighty scare,
Something that depresses me,
Something from which I wish to flee,

I might search for something anew,
from someone anew,
As you no longer exist
the way I perceived you.

***

***

46

I Hope You Don't Mind

I hope you don't mind,
I find the world beautiful,
again,
and not because of you.

I hope you don't mind
it's time we moved on
you to your dark closed spaces
me to my open sky
some place, where you won't clip my wings
lest I should spread my wings and fly.

I hope you don't mind,
But I don't want to be kind
to your devious thoughts
I'd rather wrap myself,
in the cloak of white affirmation
rather than black insecurity .

I hope you don't mind
but I realise that we are changing
Traversing in different directions
Wait of course,

You don't mind
You dark lord of despair
We can't be paired any longer
you and I.

I know you don't mind,
You never did
It was me all along.

I hope you don't mind
I'm letting you go
for I don't mind any more.

***

***

47

Lasting Summer

I'm waiting for the future to arrive.
I'm waiting to let go of my past.

So

I know I won't last the summer.
I know I won't last the summer.

I'm waiting for the light to shine,
I'm waiting for the darkness within to hide.

But

I know I won't last the summer
I know I won't last the summer

I'm waiting to be be happy
I'm waiting to smile again

Sigh

I know I won't last the summer
I know I won't last the summer

I'm waiting to forget
I'm waiting to remember

But

I know I won't last the summer
I know I won't last the summer.

I'm waiting to say goodbye to you
I'm waiting to say hello to someone new.

So
I know I won't last the summer
I know I won't last the summer.

***

***

48

Cut

If goodbyes were easy,
Then I would have said 'em long ago,
The pain is something that
I'd willingly forgo.

But, the more I wait,
The more difficult it gets until.

Restlessness seeps in,
Uncertainty hangs
by a thread
cut it yourself before someone else
does it matter
You get hurt
in the end.

CUT.

An uneasy uncertainty displaced by morbid finality.

***

***

49

I Love You Unlike

I love you unlike any other,
For I hate you and decide to leave you,
Only to return and talk to you,
Just like tutti-fruity tidbit surprises one in a bun.

I love you unlike any other,
For I do not strangle you,
Nor do I ignore you,
I love you like the in-between
Chocolate in the bourbon biscuits.

I love you unlike any other
For I cry over your hate for me
And vow that things must not be,
Only to laugh later and realise

How much I really (although awkwardly) I love thee!

***

***

50

I'm Tired

I'm tired of trying to make you learn
things that I'm meant to teach you
I must tell the angels that I can't do it any more
My minds sore
With your barging
With your constant abuse
My reds swollen with your incessant pricking,
To see if I have heart?

Do I anymore?

Drive a stake to it
It would be better
Just drive a stake to my heart
And let it flow.

Let it get blurry
and then clear
let it all disappear
in foamy white light
let me collapse,
Please no more
Please no more.

***

***

 **51**

Just One Touch

Just one more touch,
And I would have given in.
One more touch,
And I'd sink in your arms
One more plea and I'd say yes

Oh! Why did you listen to me?

My body yearns now
For your touch,
But you are now far away
All I have is a faint memory
An unsatiated feeling
A tad bit misery

Oh! Why did you listen to me?

I miss holding your hand,
Intertwining your fingers with mine,
As a prelude to a kiss and some more,
Now that would not be such a crime?

Oh! Why did you listen to me?

***

***

52

Rattlemind

What would you have me do?
Oh you'd better break my heart in two
Rather than I do that to you.

I miss you
I love you.

I missed you.
I loved you.

Of course you did.
No you didn't.
Is it my head,
Or should it be your bed
That needs the cleaning?

What kind of love is this?
Is it love?
I don't know but I do not feel it any more.
Well, neither do you.
But you are afraid,
Your loneliness will eat you into two.

Wouldn't you rather break my heart,
Into a million pieces?
Rather than stab me in the back,
Date my friend,
Say variety adds some spice.

Do it already
You coward,
Are you ready to run?
You always had a thing for
Being nude in the sun but
This time you're going to burn
And it's going to be your fault.
No one to rub suntan
While you were soaking it up.

I locked my heart
Into a tight vault,
And did the deed,
Broke myself,
Made me the fool,
Dug a grave and crawled in.
Only to spring up when least expected
Until
I'm ready to trust again.
Times change.

***

***

53

Un-Fool Me

I thought of you
And then I did again
And for a fleeting moment
I dialed you
but my brain interrupted
My heart
Longs to hear your voice
I wish I was a fool
A fool for you.
Then I wouldn't think twice
About self-respect
breaking the curse
or talking to you
while I know
you would snigger, judge and gloat
and eventually I'd be left all alone
Unhappy and directionless on a stormy sea
in a weak boat.

Instead I'll un-fool myself.
and be about my business,
And for fleeting moments
Be interrupted with kind intentions
Riddled with hope
But squashed by reality.

***

***

54

Begin Again

I do not know
What is in store
Do I even care?
While I look above
At the expansive sky
And breathe in
I think
My oh my
When will it begin
or when will it end?

I'm broken
Disillusioned
And beyond repair
In fact I do not resemble
What I was
And nobody seems
to care.

Just a faint hello
to ask me of my being
What do I tell them?
But fairy tales
of pretty darn good things.

Then they start to blame,
Point a finger to and fro
Say that love is an illusion
that one must forgo.
To live a life to the fullest
You must transcend and be free
The love, they say, that you know
Will chain thou to thee.

So while I stare at the expansive sky
and pray for a miracle of sorts
To make me transcend to living like a fool
Instead of living for naught.
For I'd rather be in love and lust
Like and adore
Trust and then lose
I'd rather die a thousand times for love
Be betrayed and cry out loud
Amidst the crowd
In the pouring rain
Rather than feel nothing
Not even this blip of pain.

***

***

55

Just like the others

You are
just like the others
But who am I to point
To hold a grudge
Against your tardiness
For I too am unclean
Washed myself time and again
with my past mistakes
And like you forgotten to put on
The dress of novelty.

You move around
Just like me
Enveloped by
your own darkness
Untouched by
the shimmering light in the distance.

I wonder, as we sit together
at a table for two
Sipping hot coffee
If like me, you too
Cling to a fleeting hope
Of brighter and better?

Where there is no past water
to dip ourselves into
If like me, do you wish
to break the chains
and be free?

Alas! The last drop of coffee touches my tongue
And just like the others, you ask
"Are you done?"
I stare at you and smile,
Just like the others I lie
Don't ask you to stay awhile
I watch you walk away
Just like the others shallow.

***

***

56

The Meet

Crystal moons spent on wired talk
Of revelry and togetherness
Vibrations carried our sentiments and desires
Across seas.
Inhibitions shed on a virtual screen
I saw and you saw me
Dreamy promises were made.
In time you said
We will meet.
Skyscrapers fell short of our expectations
And our anxiety defied infinity pools.
But desires usually find fruit
In time,
Sweaty palms made their way in an embrace,
An odd hug on a hot sunny morning and
A passionate kiss later,
Myomyhoudini
You disappeared
Like you never existed
All that remains is a sunken trunk
Of our dreams and desires
In the sea of your mouth sealed
In chains and unbreakable locks of steel.

***

***

57

Leave Him

"Leave him
I'll take care of you,"
She says
"Leave him for me"
"Don't make me choose"
I say.
I close my eyes. I've wavered already.
I look at his beautiful face almost moon kissed
He smiles. He must be dreaming.
"I can't leave him!"
I say.
I taste salt from the corner of my lips.
Always dutiful over desire
His mumblings distract me.
"He is calling"
I say.
"So am I,"
She says.
"Always"
I draw to a close the curtain
to my reflection.

Outside,
the twinkling stars play
hooky with the loony moon
brightening the swaying paisleys at the window every time
they are caught by the wind

***

***

58

I wonder

I wonder
Have I …
lost my words
along with the zigzag lines on my palm?
How now will I go-a-begging?
lost my mind
Along with my rest?
How now will I sleep?
lost my patience
With your presence?
How now will I find peace of mind?
lost myself
With you?
How now will I breathe?

***

Printed in the United States
By Bookmasters